Margaret K. McElderry Books

An imprint of Simon & Schuster Children's Publishing Division

1230 Avenue of the Americas, New York, New York 10020

Text copyright © 2007 by Karma Wilson

Illustrations copyright © 2007 by Christa Unzner

Book design by Debra Sfetsios

The text for this book is set in Didot Linotype.

The illustrations for this book are rendered in watercolor and ink.

Manufactured in China

10 9 8 7 6 5 4 3 2 1

Library of Congress Cataloging-in-Publication Data

Wilson, Karma.

Princess Me / Karma Wilson ; illustrated by Christa Unzner.

p. cm.

Summary: A little girl imagines being a princess, with her stuffed animals serving as royal subjects.

ISBN-13: 978-1-4169-4098-2

ISBN-10: 1-4169-4098-7

[1. Princesses—Fiction. 2. Toys—Fiction. 3. Imagination—Fiction. 4. Stories in rhyme.] I. Unzner-Fischer, Christa, ill. II. Title.

PZ8.3.W6976Pr 2007

[E]—dc22

2006017243

FIRST
EDITION

To Chrissy, the sweetest Princess in the land. Love, Queen Mother—K. W.

Princess Me

by karma wilson

illustrated by christa unzner

margaret k. mcelderry books   new york london toronto sydney

There is a princess in the land.

She's sweet and kind but oh-so-grand.
Forever may her kingdom stand!

Long live the Princess Me.

She wears a royal cape and crown.
She wears a fancy, frilly gown.
She hardly ever wears a frown—

she's cheerful as can be.

Her father king and mother queen,
the nicest pair you've ever seen,
are never angry, cruel, or mean,

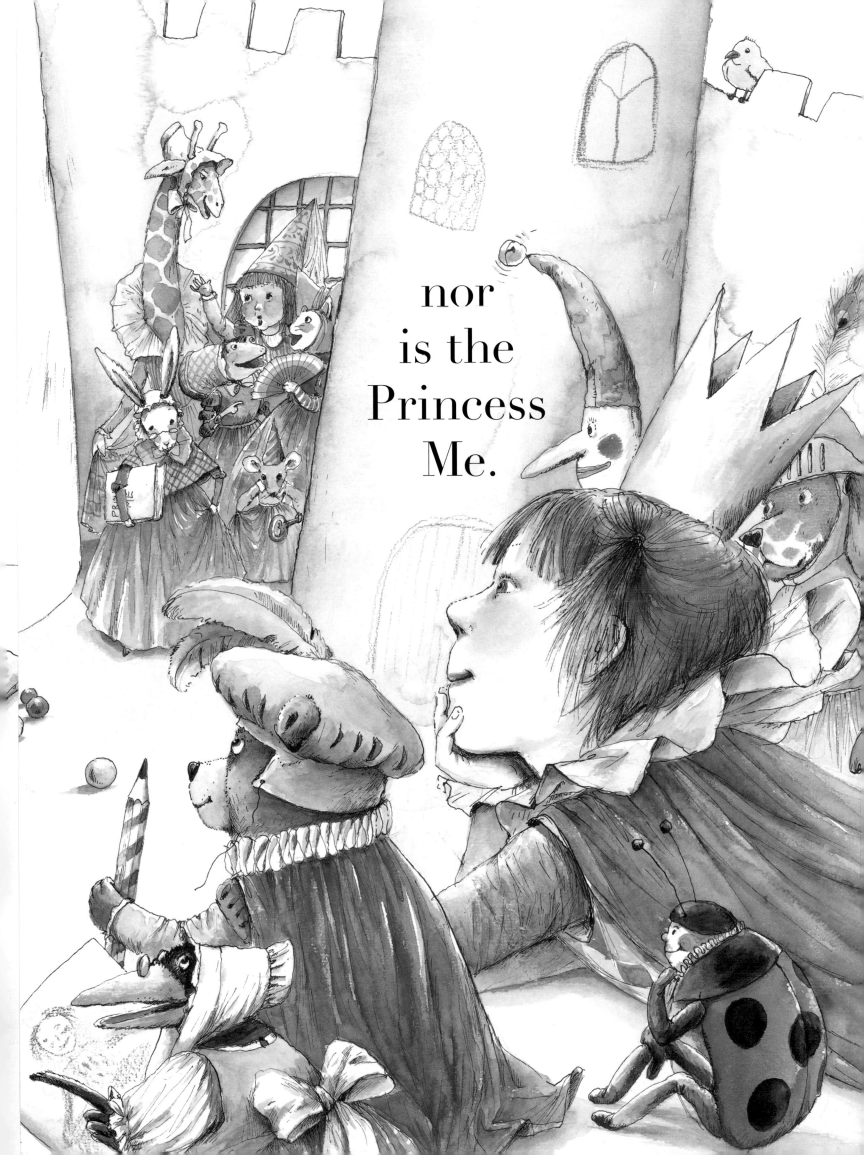

nor
is the
Princess
Me.

Her knight's the best there ever was,
and what the princess says, he does.

He's strong and brave
and true because
she rules so gracefully.

A splendid tea is set each day
and all the royal ladies stay
to chat the afternoon away

with clever Princess Me.

To all the people in her land
the princess gives to those she can.
From weakest child to strongest man,

she serves all faithfully.

Each night the king will kiss her head.
The queen will tuck her into bed.
And when the princess prayers are said,
she sleeps so peacefully.

Who is this girl?
I wonder who. . . .

Of course, my love,

IT'S
PRINCESS
YOU!